FEARLESS **FISH**

GOOF-OFF **GOOSE**

HEALTHY **HIPPO**

IMITATING **IGUANA**

JEALOUS **JACKAL**

POSITIVE **PIG**

QUESTIONING **QUAIL**

RESPONSIBLE **RABBIT**

SMARTY **STORK**

TEMPER TANTRUM **TURTLE**

HERE THEY ARE

SWEET PICKLES®

**All twenty-six of them
in stories with giggles
and tickles and awful pickles**

YAKETY **YAK**

ZANY **ZEBRA**

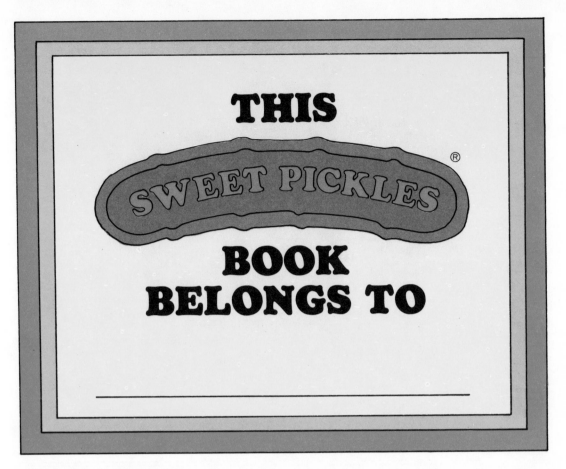

THIS

SWEET PICKLES ®

BOOK BELONGS TO

_____

In the world of *Sweet Pickles,* each animal gets into a pickle because of an all too human personality trait.

This book is about Unique Unicorn. She may be the oldest citizen in town, but she's not too old for fun.

Books in the Sweet Pickles Series:

This book is dedicated to Lilly Klopper

Library of Congress Cataloging in Publication Data

Reinach, Jacquelyn.
   Happy birthday Unicorn.

   (Sweet Pickles series)
   SUMMARY : Unicorn changes everyone's conception
of a proper birthday party for a senior citizen in
a unique way.
   [1. Unicorns—Fiction. 2. Birthdays—Fiction]
I. Title.   II. Series.
PZ7.R2747Hap   [E]   78-9585
ISBN 0-03-042066-0

Copyright © 1978 by Ruth Lerner Perle, Jacquelyn Reinach, Richard Hefter

Printed in the United States of America

Weekly Reader Books' Edition

Weekly Reader Books presents

HAPPY BIRTHDAY UNICORN

Written by Jacquelyn Reinach
Illustrated by Richard Hefter
Edited by Ruth Lerner Perle

Holt, Rinehart and Winston · New York

"Oh, no!" groaned Rabbit one morning as he looked at his calendar. "It's Unicorn's birthday next week! She's the oldest citizen in town. We have to do something about it!"

He ran to his telephone and began calling everybody.

"Oh, no!" groaned Unicorn the same morning as she looked at her calendar. "It's my birthday next week and I can feel it in my bones...just because I'm so old, they'll all think they have to give me a boring banquet. A boring banquet with boring speeches! But I'd like to have some fun!"

"Oh, no!" groaned everybody as Rabbit called them up. "Not a boring banquet with boring speeches!"

"I can't stand banquets. I can't stand speeches," grumbled Moose. "Why can't we just give her a party and have some fun?"

"We have to show proper respect," said Rabbit. "And anyway, old folks enjoy that sort of thing."

"I think Unicorn's too old for excitement," said Hippo. "It wouldn't be healthy at her age!"

"I'd like to have some excitement this year!" said Unicorn. "Not a boring banquet. And I bet they'll serve boring soft food."

"But why do we have to have boring soft food?" complained Elephant. "Why can't we have something solid, like peanut butter sandwiches and potato chips!"

"Because old folks don't eat that!" cried Rabbit. "Peanut butter sticks to their mouth. And potato chips have sharp points when you bite them!"

"Nuts!" cried Elephant. "Nuts would be delicious! And dips. Dips with chips. That would be fun for a change!"

"You know old folks don't like change," said Rabbit. "We have to stick to soft foods!"

"Oh, my, how I'd like a change for my birthday!" sighed Unicorn. "If it were up to me, I'd give a party. With peanut butter sandwiches and potato chips and nuts and all kinds of dips and chips! And music and dancing and lots of noise. And then I'd take everybody for a ride in a helicopter!"

"I wonder what I should give Unicorn for her birthday," said Quail. "Should I buy her a record? But what if she doesn't have a record player?"

"That doesn't matter," sniffed Xerus. "Old folks don't like noise, so you shouldn't buy her a record. Buy her some yarn for knitting."

"What if she doesn't knit?" asked Quail.

"Old folks *always* knit!" declared Xerus. "How else would babies get their sweaters?"

"Oh!" said Quail.

"Oh!" said Unicorn. "I can see it now. First we'll eat boring soft food and then they'll give me presents. They'll all give me yarn for knitting. And I can't stand knitting! Drats!"

Just then Zebra zipped by on his skateboard. "Happy Birthday, Unicorn!" he shouted.

"I'm not sure it's happy!" sighed Unicorn. "Things aren't what they used to be."

"What things?" asked Zebra.

"My birthdays used to be fun," said Unicorn. "I'd like to have a party. And sing and dance and whoop it up!"

"Why not?" laughed Zebra.

"But how?" said Unicorn. "If everyone wants to give me a banquet, how can I spoil their fun?"

"It's *your* birthday!" called Zebra as he skated away. "Maybe you should do what you like."

"Oh, dear!" said Unicorn.

In the park, the Unicorn Banquet Committee was having a meeting when Zebra zipped by.

"Nice day for a party!" called Zebra.

"No, it isn't!" grumbled Elephant. "It's *boring* planning speeches and soft food!"

"Yes!" smiled Zebra. "Why are you doing that?"

"Well, that's the way things have always been done!" sniffed Xerus. "Unicorn *expects* it!"

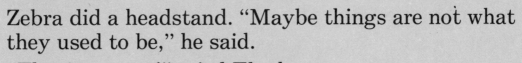

Zebra did a headstand. "Maybe things are not what they used to be," he said.

"They're worse!" cried Elephant.

"How do you know Unicorn *wants* a banquet, anyway?" giggled Zebra. "Did anybody ever ask her what *she* wants?"

"Why, no!" cried Rabbit.

"Of course not!" shouted Xerus. "Things just aren't done that way!"

"Says who?" said Zebra. He threw everybody a kiss and zipped away.

"Golly," said Pig, "maybe Zebra's right! Maybe one of us should go up to Unicorn's house and find out what *she* wants to do for her birthday."

"Okay," said Elephant. "I think Rabbit should go."

"Uh-uh!" said Rabbit. "Unicorn is our oldest and most valued customer at the bank. What if I hurt her feelings?"

"Then let's all go," said Elephant. "I'll do anything not to cook soft food. Uck!"

"Maybe Zebra's right," said Unicorn. "I really want to give a birthday party that's *fun!* So why shouldn't I tell everybody how I feel?"

Everybody on the Committee left the park and began walking up to Unicorn's house.

Unicorn collected her purse and gloves and began walking down to town.

"Goodness!" cried everybody when they saw Unicorn. "Here comes Unicorn down the hill."

"Goodness!" cried Unicorn. "Everybody's coming up the hill."

Rabbit took off his cap and gave a little bow. "Well, good afternoon, Unicorn!" he said. "We were just on our way to see you."

"And I was just on my way to see *you*!" said Unicorn. "Isn't that strange?"

"Yes, isn't it?" Rabbit took out a handkerchief and mopped his head.

They all smiled at each other. There was a long silence.

Then Zebra came skating up the block. "Happy New Year!" he shouted. "I see you all got together. Well, what's the word about the birthday celebration?"

"NO BANQUET!" shouted everybody, including Unicorn.
Everyone looked at Unicorn.
"You don't want a banquet either?" exclaimed Rabbit.
"No!" shouted Unicorn happily. "I want to have a
party! With dips and chips and music and dancing and
lots of fun!"

"You're too old for all that!" exclaimed Xerus.

"I'm not too old for fun!" said Unicorn. "And that's what I'd like to have. And I'd like to have the party at my house, if you don't mind."

"MIND?" said Elephant, beaming. "We don't mind at all!"

"Goodness!" cried Unicorn. "I'd better get busy!"

"Happy Birthday, Unicorn!" called Zebra.
"Yes!" cried Elephant happily. "Well, things
certainly aren't what they used to be!"
"No!" cried Unicorn. "They're better!"

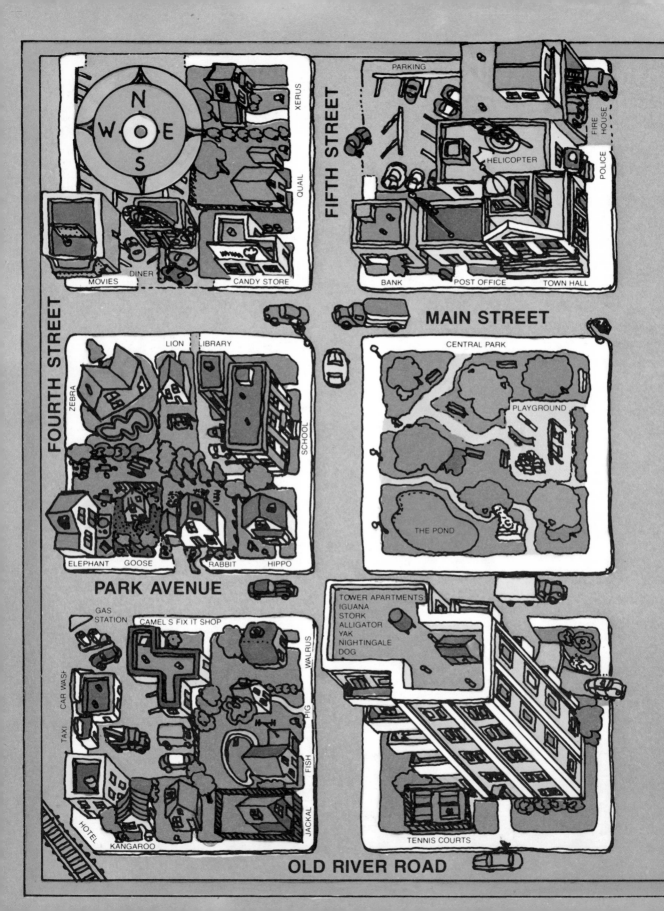